Just Custard

ReadZone Books Limited

First published in this edition 2015

© in this edition ReadZone Books Limited 2015
© in text Joe Hackett 2009
© in illustrations Alexandra Colombo 2009

Joe Hackett has asserted his right under the Copyright Designs
and Patents Act 1988 to be identified as the author of this work.

Alexandra Colombo has asserted her right under the Copyright Designs
and Patents Act 1988 to be identified as the illustrator of this work.

Every attempt has been made by the Publisher to secure appropriate
permissions for material reproduced in this book. If there has been any
oversight we will be happy to rectify the situation in future editions or
reprints. Written submissions should be made to the Publisher.

British Library Cataloguing in Publication Data (CIP) is available
for this title.

Printed in Malta by Melita Press.

ISBN 978 1 78322 167 7

Visit our website: www.readzonebooks.com

Just Custard

Joe Hackett and
Alexandra Colombo

All Duncan would eat was custard.
Just cold custard.
On its own.
From a tin.

Duncan didn't use a spoon. He drank the custard with a big red stripy straw. He slurped it between his teeth.

Slurp, slurp!

Dad took the straw away, and got quite cross.

"You're seven years old. Stop messing about," he said. "Custard isn't enough to live on."

Sitting in Mum's lap, drinking a bottle of milk, was Duncan's new baby sister, Angela. She was only a few months old.

"She's a little angel. That's why we've called her Angela," Mum told anyone who would listen.

At school, Duncan didn't eat his lunch, even though it looked delicious. He demanded custard in a tin.

Miss James asked to see Duncan alone, and talked quietly to him.

He sat in her special armchair.

"Is there anything worrying you, Duncan?" she asked.

Duncan thought for a minute.

"Yes, but it's a secret," he said, and he whispered something in her ear.

"Right," she said. "Let's see what we can do about that."

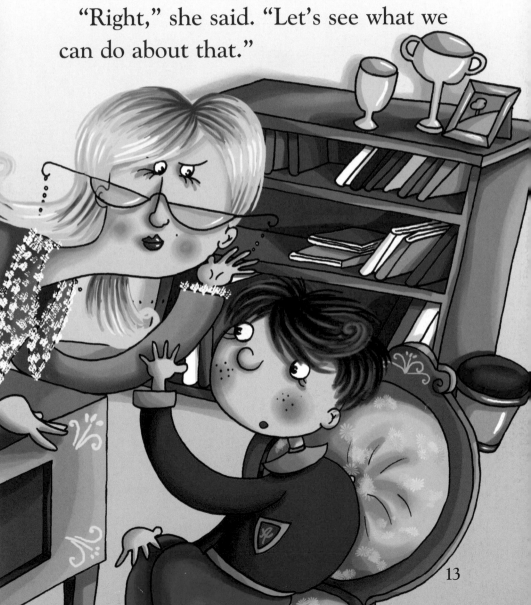

That night, at home, Duncan would still only eat custard.

Dad was so cross that he sent Duncan to his bedroom.

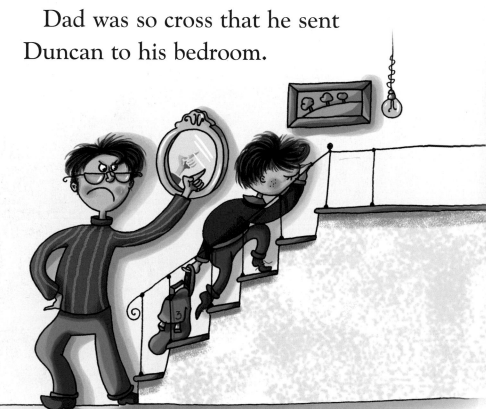

"It's not fair!" shouted Duncan. He climbed out of his bedroom window, slid down the drainpipe and ran to the park to play football with his friends.

15

But his friends weren't there and it was starting to get dark.

Duncan didn't want to go home, so he found a bench, curled up and tried to go to sleep.

Suddenly, he heard the crunch of stones underfoot. A torch beam swept backwards and forwards in the darkness, casting shadows. A man wearing a yellow coat came closer and closer.

Duncan was terrified and froze to the bench.

He screamed.

"Duncan!" shouted Dad. "Thank goodness I've found you!"

He scooped Duncan up and gave him a big cuddle. "Let's get you home, we've been so worried."

The next morning, Mum went to see
Miss James. Mum sat in her special
armchair and they had a long talk.

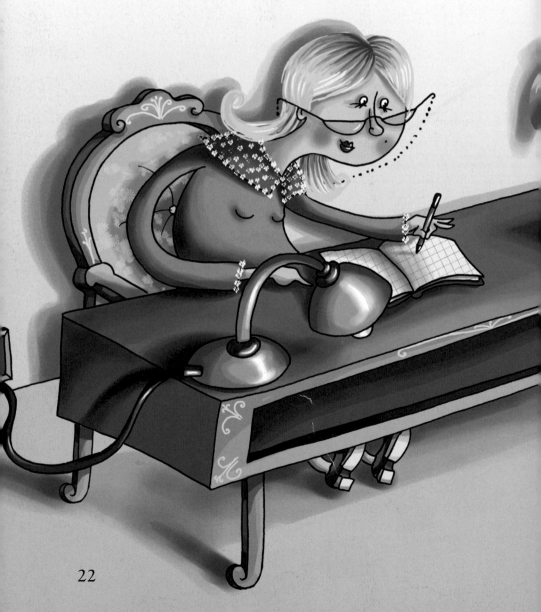

When Duncan came home from school, Mum said, "Do you think Angela might like custard too? She should be ready for something different from milk by now. Would you like to feed her?"

"Me?" asked Duncan, shocked.
No one had been allowed to feed the
Little Angel before.

Duncan dipped a plastic spoon into a pot of baby custard, and offered it to Angela.

She opened her mouth and he popped it in. He offered her another spoonful and she ate that, too. She carried on until she had finished the whole pot!

The Little Angel grinned at him, her smile covered in custard.

"She likes you, you know," Mum said.

Duncan was very, very pleased.

That night, it was chicken, peas and baked potato for tea. Afterwards, there was chocolate pudding – Duncan's favourite!

Duncan ate all his food without even being asked.

"Will you want some custard with your pudding, son?" Dad asked.

"No, thanks, Dad. Custard is just for babies!" Duncan laughed.

Did you enjoy this book?

Look out for more *Swifts* titles –
stories in 500 words

The Flamingo Who Forgot by Alan Durant and Franco Rivoli
ISBN 978 1 78322 034 2

George and the Dragonfly by Andy Blackford and Sue Mason
ISBN 978 1 78322 168 4

Glub! by Penny Little and Sue Mason
ISBN 978 1 78322 035 9

The Grumpy Queen by Valerie Wilding and Simona Sanfilippo
ISBN 978 1 78322 166 0

The King of Kites by Judith Heneghan and Laure Fournier
ISBN 978 1 78322 164 6

Hoppy Ever After by Alan Durant and Sue Mason
ISBN 978 1 78322 036 6

Just Custard by Joe Hackett and Alexandra Colombo
ISBN 978 1 78322 167 7

Space Cadets to the Rescue by Paul Harrison and Sue Mason
ISBN 978 1 78322 039 7

Monster in the Garden by Anne Rooney and Bruno Robert
ISBN 978 1 78322 163 9

Wait a Minute, Ruby! by Mary Chapman and Nick Schon
ISBN 978 1 78322 165 3

The One That Got Away by Paul Harrison and Tim Archbold
ISBN 978 1 78322 037 3

The Perfect Prince by Paul Harrison and Sue Mason
ISBN 978 1 78322 038 0